Dear Parent:
Your child's love of reading

Every child learns to read in a different way
You can help your young reader improve an
by encouraging his or her own interests and abilities. You can also guide your child's spiritual development by reading stories with biblical values and Bible stories, like I Can Read! books published by Zonderkidz. From books your child reads with you to the first books he or she reads alone, there are I Can Read! books for every stage of reading:

SHARED READING
Basic language, word repetition, and whimsical illustrations, ideal for sharing with your emergent reader.

BEGINNING READING
Short sentences, familiar words, and simple concepts for children eager to read on their own.

READING WITH HELP
Engaging stories, longer sentences, and language play for developing readers.

READING ALONE
Complex plots, challenging vocabulary, and high-interest topics for the independent reader.

ADVANCED READING
Short paragraphs, chapters, and exciting themes for the perfect bridge to chapter books.

I Can Read! books have introduced children to the joy of reading since 1957. Featuring award-winning authors and illustrators and a fabulous cast of beloved characters, I Can Read! books set the standard for beginning readers.

A lifetime of discovery begins with the magical words **"I Can Read!"**

Visit www.icanread.com for information on enriching your child's reading experience.
Visit www.zonderkidz.com for more Zonderkidz I Can Read! titles.

The law that brings respect for the LORD is pure.
It lasts forever. The directions the LORD gives
are true. All of them are completely right.
They are more priceless than gold. They have greater
value than huge amounts of pure gold. They are
sweeter than honey that is taken from the honeycomb.
—*Psalm 19:9–10*

Mrs. Rosey Posey and Hidden Treasure
Text copyright © 2008 by Robin's Ink, LLC
Illustrations copyright © 2008 by Christina Schofield

Requests for information should be addressed to:
Zonderkidz, *Grand Rapids, Michigan 49530*

Library of Congress Cataloging-in-Publication Data

Gunn, Robin Jones, 1955-
    [Mrs. Rosey-Posey and the treasure hunt]
    Mrs. Rosey Posey and the hidden treasure / story by Robin Jones Gunn ;
pictures by Christina Schofield.
        p. cm. -- (I can read! Level 2)
    Summary: A treasure hunt in and around Mrs. Rosey-Posey's house leads
Ross, Jacob, and Adam to their own copies of the Bible, the greatest treasure
of all time.
    ISBN: 978-0-310-71577-1 (softcover)
    [1. Treasure hunt (Game)--Fiction. 2. Bible--Fiction. 3. Christian life--Fiction.]
I. Schofield, Christina (Christina Diane), 1972- ill. II. Title.
PZ7.G972Mqh 2008
[E]--dc22

2007034321

All Scripture quotations unless otherwise noted are taken from the *Holy Bible: New
International Reader's Version*®. NIrV®. Copyright © 1995, 1996, 1998 by International
Bible Society. Used by permission of Zondervan. All rights reserved.

Published in association with the Books & Such Literary Agency, 52 Mission Circle,
Suite 122, PMB 170, Santa Rosa, California 95409-5370, www.bookandsuch.biz

Zonderkidz is a trademark of Zondervan.

Editor: Betsy Flikkema
Art direction: Jody Langley
Cover design: Sarah Molegraaf

Printed in the United States of America

08 09 10 11 12 • 5 4 3 2 1

Mrs. Rosey Posey
and the
Hidden Treasure

story by Robin Jones Gunn

pictures by Christina Schofield

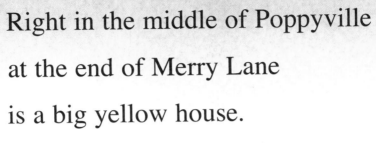

Right in the middle of Poppyville

at the end of Merry Lane

is a big yellow house.

Mrs. Rosey Posey lives here.

Children love Mrs. Rosey Posey.

Poppyville

One sunny day, Ross, Jacob, and Adam
dressed like pirates and climbed
into Mrs. Rosey Posey's tree house.

"Captain, Captain!" Jacob cried.

"Ship on the port side."

Mrs. Rosey Posey called up,

"Ahoy, matey!

I brought books and apples."

"Thank ye kindly," said Ross.

He pulled the bucket on board.

The boys opened the books.

A map fell out of Adam's book.

"What is that?" asked Jacob.

The boys looked at the paper.

"It's a treasure map," said Adam.

"Let's follow the clues," said Ross.

"Look!" said Ross.

"Here is the tree house.

The arrow points to the pond."

"Then let's go!" said Jacob.

"Let's find the treasure."

The boys ran to the pond.

"Now where?" asked Adam.

"The map points to the back door,"
Ross said. "Let's go there."

He turned the map over.

"Look! A clue," said Ross.

"A treasure sweet.

Open it up, adventures meet."

"That means the treasure is food,"
said Jacob.

Mrs. Rosey Posey opened the door.

She said, "It's my pirate friends!

What brings ye to my galley?"

"A treasure map," Ross said.

"Where do we go now?" said Adam.

Mrs. Rosey Posey looked at the map.

"Upstairs to a small door," she said.

"Follow me," said Ross.

Adam and Jacob ran upstairs.

So did Mrs. Rosey Posey.

They saw a small door.

"What is in there?" they asked.

"It's a special slide for pirates,"
said Mrs. Rosey Posey.

The pirates slid down one by one.

"Wheee!" they all said.

"Where do we go now?" Adam asked.

"Outside," said Jacob.

The boys looked at the map.

"Look for a chest," said Ross.

"I found it," said Jacob.

Inside they found three books

with a candy bar on top.

"It's a treasure sweet!" said Ross.

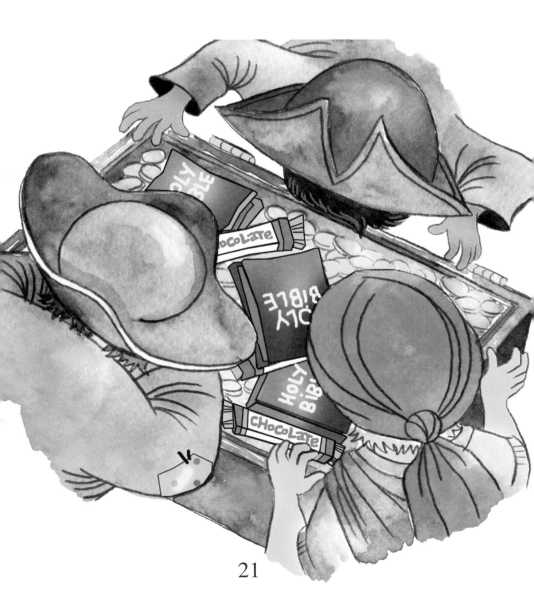

They ran to show their Bibles
to Mrs. Rosey Posey.

"You found the greatest treasure,"

she said.

"Did you know that God's Word

is worth more than gold

and is sweeter than honey?"

said Mrs. Rosey Posey.

"Just like our clue!" said Adam.

"Aye, matey!" said Mrs. Rosey Posey.

"Our clue read, 'A treasure sweet.

Open it up, adventures meet.'

What's the adventure?" asked Ross.

Mrs. Rosey Posey smiled.

Her eyes had a twinkle.

Her smile had a zing.

Mrs. Rosey Posey had a secret.

"Right here in the Bible," she said,
"there are stories about giants
and kings and talking donkeys."

"Are the stories true?" asked Adam.

"Indeed," said Mrs. Rosey Posey.

"Every word is true."

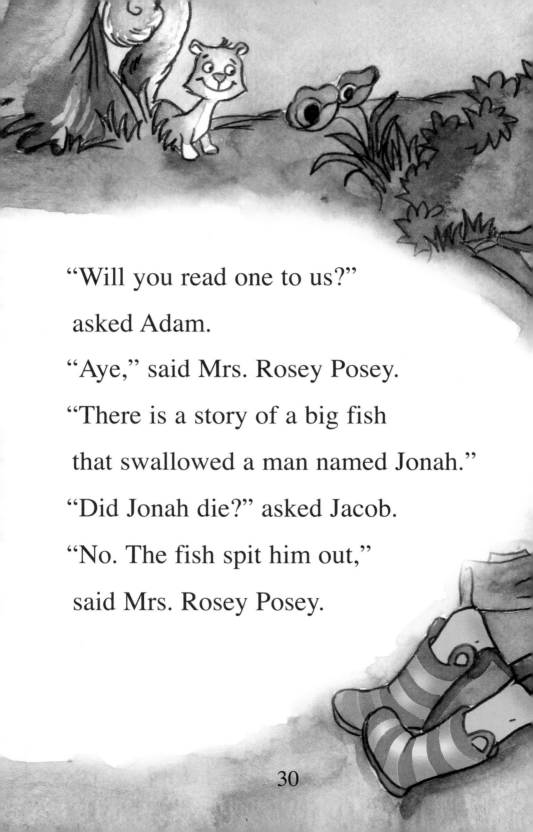

"Will you read one to us?"
asked Adam.

"Aye," said Mrs. Rosey Posey.

"There is a story of a big fish
that swallowed a man named Jonah."

"Did Jonah die?" asked Jacob.

"No. The fish spit him out,"
said Mrs. Rosey Posey.

"Cool," said Adam.

"Way cool," said Jacob.

"Read that one first," said Ross.

So Mrs. Rosey Posey did.

The pirates lifted their eye patches.

It helped them to hear much better.